POST CARD

This space for Address only

Lost Toys Returned

Townspeople are delighted by the surprising return of flying discs lost on rooftops and kites tangled high in treetops. Balls and other toys long since lost began to reappear in the yards of Pfeffernut County children a few weeks back. At first, no one knew just how these things were being returned from their high places. Then a local girl spotted a lanky farmhand named Louie as he plucked two baseballs from the gutters of her family's home.

"I couldn't believe my eyes," she said. "He's nearly as tall as the water tower."

"Aw, it's nothing," Louie said. "When I see those poor toys stuck where most folks can't reach, I feel real sorry. I can't help but reach down and put them back where they belong."

Please see LOUIE, Page A2

...ally thought ...a local far... ...ng basketbal...

...ot sure w... ...e great th...

scho... ...County... Pfeffernut... ...fernut had high hopes for Louie.

family picnic

FRIENDS

Greetings from Pfeffernut County

Pfeffernut Book Fair $1

Pfeffernut Book Fair $1

Grandpa at fishing hole

Pfeffernuese Cookies - 5 dozen

4 C. flour   1/2 C. butter
1/2 tsp. ground nutmeg   1/2 tsp. cinnamon
1/2 C. white sugar   2 eggs
3/4 C. light molasses   1/2 tsp. ground cloves
1 1/4 tsp. baking soda   1/3 C. powdered sugar

Stir together flour, sugar, baking soda,
spices + dash black pepper. Melt molasses
+ butter in saucepan, cool.

with an egg, add dry ingredients
to molasses mixture, mix well, cover
chill for several hours. Place on
shape into 1" balls. Bake at 350°
cookie sheet. Bake at 350 until cookie's
12 to 14 minutes or until cookies
done. Cool. Roll in powdered sugar

HENRY SHORTBULL

Swallows the Sun

by Jill Kalz

illustrated by Sahin Erkocak

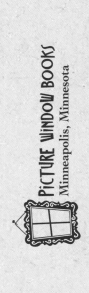

PICTURE WINDOW BOOKS
Minneapolis, Minnesota

Special thanks to our story consultant:
Terry Flaherty, Ph.D. Professor of English
Minnesota State University, Mankato

Editor: Christianne Jones
Designer: Tracy Davies
Page Production: Melissa Kes
Art Director: Nathan Gassman
The illustrations in this book were
created digitally.

Picture Window Books
5115 Excelsior Boulevard
Suite 232
Minneapolis, MN 55416
877-845-8392
www.picturewindowbooks.com

Library of Congress Cataloging-in-Publication Data
Kalz, Jill.
Henry Shortbull swallows the sun / by Jill Kalz ; illustrated by
Sahin Erkocak.
p. cm. — (Pfeffernut County)
Summary: Greedy Henry Shortbull wants to have everything in the
whole world, but when he swallows the sun one day, he realizes that he
has gone too far.
ISBN-13: 978-1-4048-3695-2 (hardcover)
ISBN-10: 1-4048-3695-0 (hardcover)
[1. Greed—Fiction. 2. Sun—Fiction.] I. Erkocak, Sahin, ill. II. Title.
PZ7.K12655He 2007
[E]—dc22
2007004033

In memory of my grandma, Sally Hartl — J.K.

WELCOME TO PFEFFERNUT

Pfeffernut County is a friendly little place on the prairie. It's full of kind people who dream big. Funny things have a way of happening here. Get ready for some new adventures, and enjoy your visit. We're sure glad you stopped by.

Henry Shortbull didn't have a middle name. But he wanted one. And it wasn't just a middle name he wanted. He wanted more—of everything.

He wanted more toys, more candy, more EVERYTHING.
If Henry Shortbull had a middle name, it would have been
Greedy—Henry Greedy Shortbull.

On the school bus, Henry wouldn't let anyone sit with him. Sometimes, he even lay across the aisle like a fallen tree, blocking the whole back of the bus.

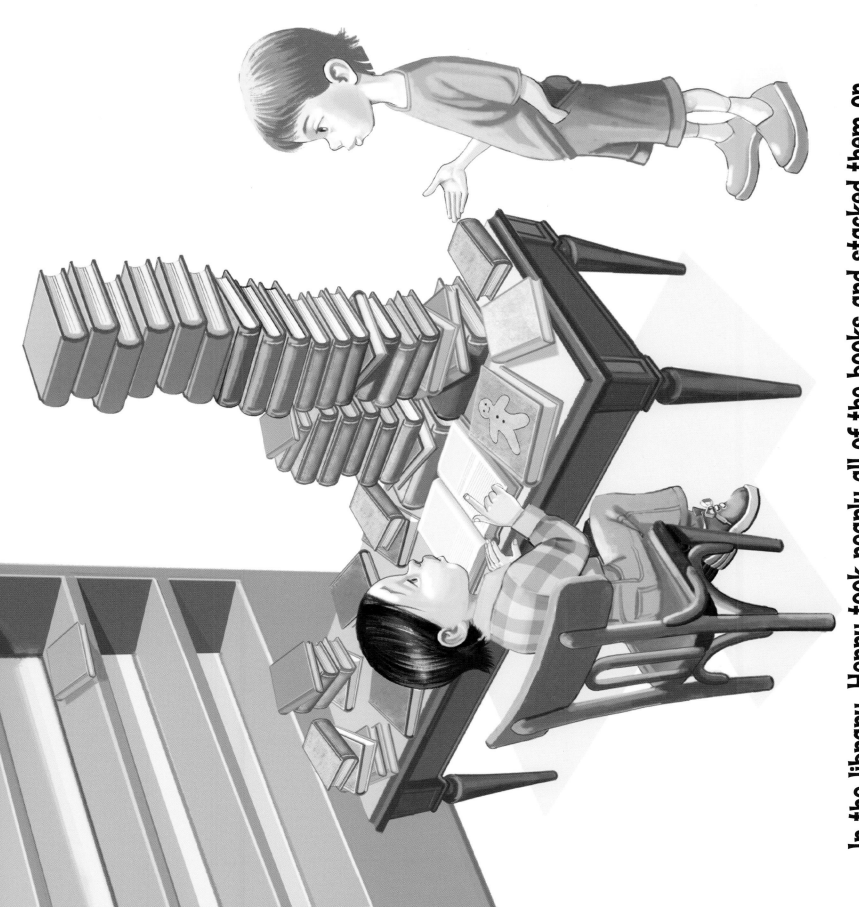

In the library, Henry took nearly all of the books and stacked them on his table. When someone asked to borrow one, Henry shook his head. "No," he said, "I'm reading all of these, all at once. You'll have to wait."

In the band room, Henry stuffed his pockets with bells, rattles, and whistles. He grabbed the cymbals, the bongos, and all of the drumsticks. He wore a tambourine like a crown.

At birthday parties, Henry hogged the cake and ice cream. At the movies, he munched on the biggest tub of popcorn. And on Christmas Day, he wrapped his arms around his little sisters' presents (even the frilly dolls he really didn't want) and cried, "MINE!"

But Henry Shortbull still wanted more.

One summer day, Henry biked down to the fishing hole.
The sun shone brightly off the water. Henry squinted.
He felt the sun's warmth on his skin.

And just like that, Henry Shortbull knew what he had to do.
He climbed the tallest tree he could find, plucked the sun
from the sky, and—GULP!—swallowed it whole.

After all, what did everything in the world need? The sun!
So if Henry had the sun, he had everything, right?

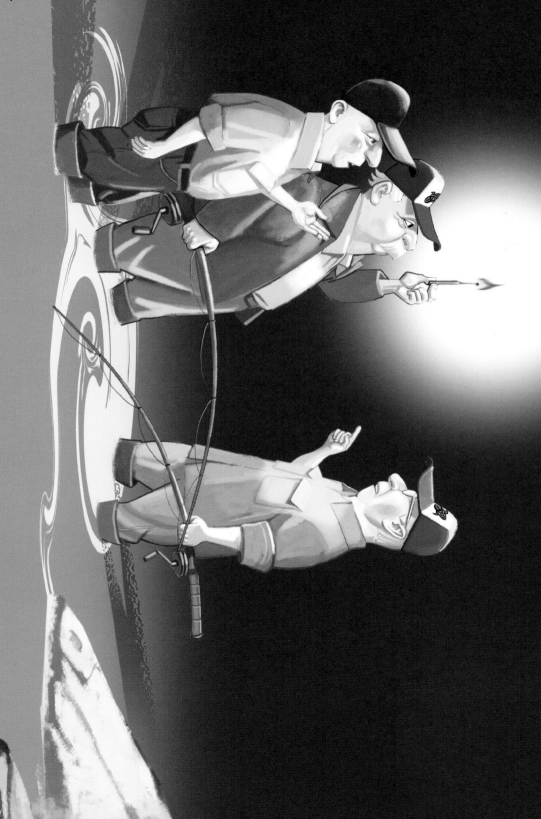

In a blink, the light was gone. Henry heard the fishermen groan. One of the men lit a match.

"It's like the sun's batteries died," the first fisherman said.

"Or like someone took a deep breath and blew it out," the second one said.

The third fisherman sighed and said, "It's like the sun packed up and moved far, far away."

None of them suspected little Henry Shortbull.

The worried townspeople turned on every bulb they could find. They even looped strings of Christmas lights around the buildings on Main Street.

When the power ran out, the townspeople lit candles, lamps, and lanterns. Shy, flickering lights dotted the sidewalks and street corners.

Henry stood in the shadows and watched. His stomach started to rumble. It started to twitch.

Finally a cold wind blew through. It froze birds in mid-flight and cats in mid-scratch. It even froze cows in mid-moo.

"Oh, what will we do?" the townspeople cried.

Henry's stomach grumbled a terrible grumble. There was no time to waste.

Back home, Henry mumbled, "I'm sorry. I never should have swallowed it."

"Swallowed what?" his grandmother asked.

"I wanted everything, so I swallowed the sun," Henry said. "But now everyone is sad. And I have nothing to do and nowhere to go. I have nothing!"

His grandmother smiled. "Oh, Henry," she said. "You have your family. Having people who love you is worth more than 20 suns."

And just like that, Henry Shortbull knew what he had to do. He ran into the shed and grabbed his father's tallest ladder. He climbed to the top, opened his arms, and closed his eyes.

He thought about his family, his neighbors, and his classmates. Henry thought about everything, except Henry. With each thought, his stomach glowed brighter and brighter. It buzzed and bubbled and burbled and then . . .

Henry burped.

Sunlight filled the sky and spilled onto the ground. The townspeople saw the sun glowing high above them. They saw a happy boy on a ladder. And they saw a smiling grandmother standing in the yard.

"That's my good boy," she said. "That's my Henry Shortbull."

And just like that, the little boy with no middle name didn't want one anymore. He knew he already had everything he needed.

Henry Shortbull had more than enough.

PFEFFERNUT FOLLOW-UP

1. Henry Shortbull is a very greedy boy at the beginning of the story. Do you know someone who is greedy? What kinds of greedy things has he or she done?

2. The opposite of being greedy is being generous. Generous people happily share their time, money, and things with others. How are you generous at home? At school? In your neighborhood?

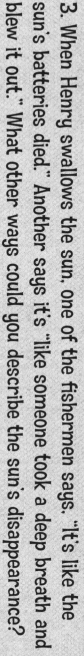

3. When Henry swallows the sun, one of the fishermen says, "It's like the sun's batteries died." Another says it's "like someone took a deep breath and blew it out." What other ways could you describe the sun's disappearance?

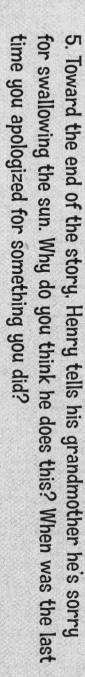

4. Henry swallows the sun because he thinks that by doing so, he'll have everything in the world. Would you want to have everything in the world? Why or why not?

5. Toward the end of the story, Henry tells his grandmother he's sorry for swallowing the sun. Why do you think he does this? When was the last time you apologized for something you did?

Fun Sun Facts

• The sun is considered an average-sized star compared to other stars in the universe. But it is still very large.

• The sun is about 4.5 billion years old. Most scientists believe that the sun will burn for another 5 billion years before it runs out of fuel.

• The sun's temperature ranges from 10,832 degrees Fahrenheit (6,000 degrees Celsius) on the coolest points of the surface to 59,000,000° F (32,777,727° C) at the sun's core. Most ovens reach only 500° F (260° C).

• The sun is nearly 93 million miles (149 million kilometers) from Earth. If you could drive a car from Earth to the sun, it would take about 193 years, driving 55 miles (88 km) per hour.

• The speed of light is 186,000 miles (297,600 km) per second. At that rate, an airplane could circle Earth seven and a half times in just one second!

The series title, "Pfeffernut County," comes from the German word *Pfeffernuesse* (FEFF-er-noos). Pfeffernuesse are German spice cookies that are popular around Christmastime. They get their spicy flavor from ingredients such as cinnamon, nutmeg, cloves, and black pepper.

Pfeffernut County Times

50¢ weekdays $1.00 Sundays

More Books to Read

Asch, Frank. *The Sun Is My Favorite Star.* San Diego: Harcourt Brace, 2000.

Kleven, Elisa. *Sun Bread.* New York: Dutton Children's Books, 2001.

Root, Phyllis. *Lucia and the Light.* Cambridge, Mass.: Candlewick Press, 2006.

Seuss, Dr. *How the Grinch Stole Christmas.* New York: Random House, 1957.

FactHound

All of the sites on FactHound have been researched by our staff.

FactHound offers a safe, fun way to find Web sites related to topics in this book.

1. Visit *www.facthound.com*
2. Type in this special code: 1404836950
3. Click on the FETCH IT button.

Your trusty FactHound will fetch the best sites for you!

Look for all of the books in the Pfeffernut County series:

Farmer Cap
Fawn Braun's Big City Blues
Henry Shortbull Swallows the Sun
Louie the Layabout

Granapa at fishing hole

Greetings from
Pfeffernut County

Pfeffernut Book Fair $1

Pfeffernut Book Fair $1

Pfeffernese Cookies - 5 dozen

½ c. butter

4 c. flour
½ tsp. ground nutmeg ½ tsp. cinnamon
½ c. white sugar 2 eggs
½ c. light molasses ½ tsp. ground cloves
¾ c. light molasses ⅓ c. powdered sugar
1 ¼ tsp. baking soda

Stir together flour, sugar, baking soda,
spices + dash black pepper. cool. Melt molasses
+ butter in saucepan, cool. add dry ingredients,
stir in eggs, add, mix well, cover
to molasses mixture. chill for several hours.
chill for several hours. Place on
shape into 1" balls. Bake at 350°
cookie sheet. Bake 8 until cookie
12 to 14 minutes or until done.
done. Cool. Roll in powdered sugar

The Cows Cannot Mooove Along

Pfeffernut County has not seen the sun for three straight days. Weather forecasters have no idea what's going on. The local livestock is completely frozen. Cows are no longer producing milk, just ice cream. Will this deep freeze continue, or will the sun shine down on Pfeffernut again?

PFEFFERNUT

Pfeffernut Theater Grand Reopening

Downtown Pfeffernut looked more like New York City than a small town on Friday night. Bright lights glared, loud music blared, and huge crowds poured into the local theater to celebrate its grand reopening.

Main Street, minutes before the Theater's Grand...

Last summer, a huge tornado destroyed the theater. Staying true to

Pfeffernut form, the owner picked a fitting movie to be shown at the reo... "Twister." Please see TH...

harvest time

Local Farmer Gets Pilot's License

Farmer Cap of Pfeffernut County endured many hours in

School Book Drive a Colorful Success!

A small bet between the principal and students at Pfeffernut Elementary School has led to the largest book drive in the school's history. The students collected 1,000 books in just one week.

"We challenged our students, and they made us proud," the principal said. "Now I have to fulfill my part of the bet and dye my hair blue for the rest of the school year."

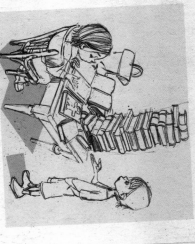